U0023371

閃亮點
ENRICH SPOT

丁丁企鵝遊學館

有情有境學英語

學英語　01　情緒篇 Emotions

原作　江記　·　撰文　閱亮點編輯室

Contents
目錄

Meet the characters
角色介紹

Ding Ding
A little penguin.
He is a lively kid who is
ready to play at all times!

Mum
Ding Ding's mother.
She always teaches Ding Ding
to be a well-behaved child.

Mushroom

A friend of Ding Ding.
Her hairstyle makes her
look like a mushroom!

Glasses

Another friend.
He always wears
a pair of glasses.

Ryan

Ding Ding's cousin.
He is a mature penguin
for his age.

Masihung

A bear who wears a mask on his face.
He goes beyond lazy and
into super lazy!

Panda

A roommate of Masihung.
He is a conscientious panda. Sadly,
he is worlds apart from Masihung.

How are you feeling? 你感覺如何？

Can you tell what Ding Ding is feeling by looking at each face?

Happy 開心

Excited 興奮

Surprised 驚訝

Sad 傷心

ARRRRGH!

Angry 生氣

Shy 害羞

Scared 害怕

Bored 無聊

Satisfied 滿意

Confused 混亂

Grumpy 煩躁

Helpless 無奈

Talking about feelings
談談你的感覺

When you have any feelings, you can tell me.

Let's see… I feel hungry.

Well, I'm talking about emotions.

1 Let's see. 讓我想想。

2 Emotion 情緒

Happy 開心

1 Good mood 好心情

2 Glad 愉快

3 Be over the moon 欣喜若狂

4 Walk on air 高興得飄飄然

Happy 開心

1 Good mood 好心情

2 Glad 愉快

3 Be over the moon 欣喜若狂

4 Walk on air 高興得飄飄然

◯ Never better! 非常開心呢！

1 How are you doing? 你好嗎？　　**2** Just kidding. 開玩笑而已。

Having fun with friends!
跟朋友一起玩！

1 Fantastic! 好極！ **2** Together 一起 **3** Join in 加入

13

Excited 興奮

1 Thrilled 太興奮了

2 Yippee! 嘩！太好啦！

3 Look forward to 期待

4 Can't stop 禁不住

When you are excited...
興奮的時候

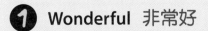 **1** Wonderful 非常好　　**2** Joy 喜悅

Proud 驕傲

1 My turn. 輪到我了。

2 Hold on. 等一下。

3 Be fair! 公平一點吧！

Feeling loved 感受到愛

I'm contented with my friends around...

...because I know they like me as I am.

I love being loved. What about you?

1 Contented 滿足

2 Like me as I am 喜愛真正的我

Shy 害羞

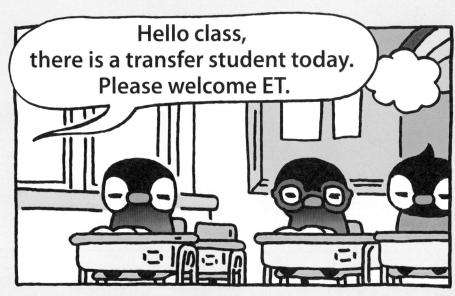

1. **Transfer student** 轉校生

2. **Welcome** 歡迎

3. **Blush** 臉紅

When you are shy...
害羞的時候

1 Break the ice　打破沉默

2 Same here.　我也一樣。

Lonely 孤單

I feel isolated. Nobody cares about me...

Sobbing...

1 Isolated 孤立

2 Care 關心

3 Sob 啜泣

4 Hug 擁抱

Sad 傷心

1 Out of sorts 心情煩惱

2 Feel down 悶悶不樂

3 Bad mood 壞心情

4 Feel blue 沮喪

Why do you feel sad?
你為甚麼傷心？

Ding Ding is crying all day long.

Waa... waa...

Mushroom has moved to another place. I'm really sad.

It's for you, Ding Ding.

Mushroom?

...

?!

Ha-ha! We'll see at school tomorrow.

1 All day long 一整天

2 It's for you. （這電話）找你的。

The sky is crying too.
天空也哭了！

1 A long face 愁眉苦臉

2 ACHOO! 乞嗤！（打噴嚏的聲音）

Cheer up! 振作一點！

1 Blubber 放聲哭泣

2 Pull yourself together. 振作起來。

I'm breathing fire.

I want to scream.

What is this feeling?

Hey, this is angry.

1 Breathe fire
噴火（非常生氣）

2 Scream 尖叫

When you are angry...
生氣的時候

Stop making fun of me! I'm really annoyed!

Ouch! It hurts!

Stop! Feeling angry doesn't mean you can throw things or beat someone.

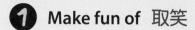 **1** Make fun of 取笑　　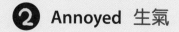 **2** Annoyed 生氣

Keep calm and carry on
保持冷靜，繼續努力

Don't get too annoyed! Take a deep breath and try to calm down.

And bounce up and down on the sofa to release.

1 Calm down 冷靜下來

2 Sofa 沙發

3 Release 發洩

Fight 吵架

1 Heartbroken 非常傷心

2 I didn't mean it. 我無心的。

Fussy kid 愛鬧情緒的孩子

1 Humph! 哼！

2 Sulk 發脾氣

3 Corner 角落

① Play 話劇

② Disappointing 令人失望

Scared 害怕

Please don't do this. The piggy bank is shivering.

But I need to break it to buy a new game…

1 Piggy bank 小豬錢箱

2 Shiver 發抖

3 Cold sweat 冷汗

Ding Ding looks so scary. I'm afraid of him.

My heart beats so loud.

I broke out into a cold sweat.

Jealous 妒忌

This book seems interesting. I want to have it for myself.

You have lots of books. Try to cherish the things you have.

1 Have it for myself 自己擁有 **2** Cherish 珍惜

Worried 擔心

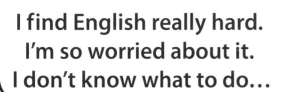

I find English really hard.
I'm so worried about it.
I don't know what to do…

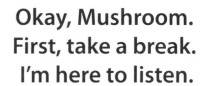

Okay, Mushroom.
First, take a break.
I'm here to listen.

Am I comforting her well?
This is worrying me so much.

❶ Take a break 休息一會

❷ Comfort 安慰

Nervous 緊張

1 Sweaty 流汗的

2 Tremble 緊張顫抖

3 Vomit 嘔吐

4 Take it easy. 放鬆點。

Shocked 嚇一跳

1. Oh, my! 噢，天啊！

2. Mistake 錯誤

3. Accident 意外

Bored 無聊

Everybody feels bored from time to time.

When you feel bored...

Hee-hee.

I like it.

It's nice to have a companion.

1 From time to time 有時

2 Companion 好伙伴

Let's play game! 齊來玩遊戲！

1 Make a face 扮鬼臉

2 Come on 快點

Let's make a face.

Come on, it's fun!

It's good to make people laugh.

丁丁企鵝遊學館

有情有境
學英語 01 情緒篇 Emotion

原作	江記（江康泉）
撰文	閱亮點編輯室
內容總監	曾玉英
責任編輯	Zeny Lam & Hockey Yeung
顧問編輯	Pray Eucha
書籍設計	Stephen Chan

出版	閱亮點有限公司 Enrich Spot Limited
	九龍觀塘鴻圖道 78 號 17 樓 A 室
發行	天窗出版社有限公司 Enrich Publishing Ltd.
	九龍觀塘鴻圖道 78 號 17 樓 A 室
電話	(852) 2793 5678
傳真	(852) 2793 5030
網址	www.enrichculture.com
電郵	info@enrichculture.com
出版日期	2021 年 7 月初版

| 承印 | 嘉昱有限公司 |
| | 九龍新蒲崗大有街 26-28 號天虹大廈 7 字樓 |

定價	港幣 $88　新台幣 $440
國際書號	978-988-75704-1-7
圖書分類	(1) 兒童圖書　　(2) 英語學習

版權所有　不得翻印
All Rights Reserved

©2021 Enrich Spot Limited
Published & Printed in Hong Kong

TM

DING DING

ding_ding_penguin